# SARA AND THE MOONLIGHT RESCUE

## THE ITURIA CHRONICLES

## J.B. MOONSTAR

BOOK 11

# SARA AND THE MOONLIGHT RESCUE

## THE ITURIA CHRONICLES

J.B. MOONSTAR

Published By: The Little Horsemen an imprint of 4 Horsemen Publications, Inc.

The Little Horsemen Publications
℅ 4 Horsemen Publications, Inc.
PO Box 419
Sylva, NC 28779
4horsemenpublications.com
info@4horsemenpublications.com

Cover &Illustration by Jenn Kotick.
Contact for commssions at Jkotickart@gmail.com .
Typesetting by Autumn Skye
Editor Laura Mita



*Library of Congress Control Number: 2023947027*

*Paperback ISBN: 979-8-8232-0346-3*
*Hardcover ISBN: 979-8-8232-0347-0*
*Audio ISBN: 979-8-8232-0348-7*
*Digital ISBN: 979-8-8232-0349-4*

# DEDICATION

This book is dedicated to Allison Skidmore and her organization, Leave Them Wild, for all the work they do to save the lives of wild tigers from the many dangers they face at the hands of humans. Thank you for your courage and dedication to protect these magnificent creatures!

# Dear Reader,

In my continuing chronicles of Ituria's Alliance, I am relaying a story of a daring moonlight rescue by Sara and her new friend Megan. When learning of a group of poached tiger cubs being transported to a tiger farm, Megan seeks out Sara's help to come to their rescue. Under the light of a full moon, they plan the rescue, and with Angela's help, they venture deep into dangerous unfamiliar territory to achieve their goal—save the baby tigers before they are delivered to the tiger farm!

Join Sara, the newest member of Ituria's Alliance, as she accepts another mission to save innocent tiger cubs. With close calls and narrow escapes, Sara and Megan must use all items at their disposal to succeed; but will it be enough to outwit the poachers?

Sincerely,

*Knocker,*
First Guard to Ituria

# Table of Contents

# Chapter One

# A VISITOR ARRIVES

The sound of owls hooting outside the house kept Sara company as she lay in bed. She had been tossing and turning for at least an hour, wide awake. Both her brother and father were asleep as they had to get up early in the morning to go to work for the lumber company. Her mind kept racing back to the talk she overheard at the market earlier today about changes being made, new rules that were being enforced by the local authorities: no one allowed out at night, no contact with strangers, report anyone who is not a resident to the authorities!

Listening quietly to the conversations she heard without reacting or responding, she knew why this change was happening. Several weeks ago, she and her new friend Knocker rescued several young tiger cubs from the local poacher gang. Now the poachers were determined to find the teenage boy who had broken curfew the night the cubs disappeared. While they didn't have any evidence that he was connected to the theft, they wanted to find him for questioning.

Smiling to herself, she remembered Knocker's role in the rescue and how he managed to save all the cubs, getting them to a safe place on Ituria's Island, where they would not be hunted by humans. Glad to play a part in their rescue, she felt proud when Knocker told her that she was now a part of Ituria's Alliance, a group dedicated to protecting and rescuing animals in need. Knocker said he would contact her again if he needed her assistance in the area.

The night of the tiger cub rescue was also when she discovered the necklace her father gave her contained the spirit of Angela, the ghost of a tiger who was killed by poachers many months ago. Angela's spirit stayed in the forest when her claw broke off and fell to the ground during her struggle with the poachers. Finding Angela's claw, Sara's father made it into a necklace and gave it to Sara. He told her it would protect her from evil, but she must not let anyone know she had the necklace.

Angela had reached out to Sara that fateful evening, connecting her to a wounded tiger mother's cries for help so that Sara could learn where the cubs were hiding and rescue them. Since then, Angela had been a comforting companion, helping to keep her calm as the poachers got more demanding and menacing to the commoners in the village.

Wrapping her fingers gently around the necklace, Sara wondered if she would ever hear from Knocker again. While she was afraid of the poachers, her willingness to help rescue threatened animals gave her the courage to overcome her fear. Sara's mother had told her to take care of herself, and she knew that she also needed to take care of others who needed her help.

"Sara," Angela's voice softly called to her, "there is someone calling for you. The voice says they are a friend of Knocker's." Only Sara could hear Angela, her voice became part of Sara's thoughts.

Sitting up quickly, she answered back, "Who is it? Where are they now?"

"They are out in the woods behind the house," Angela replied in Sara's mind. "They cannot approach for fear of being seen. They ask that you come out into the backyard to meet them."

"Angela," Sara whispered, "do you know who they are? Should we trust them?"

"Let me listen and see who it might be," Angela answered. "I will contact the spirit of the owls to identify who might be calling for you."

Holding the claw necklace close, Sara waited for Angela to reach out to the owls. After hearing several series of "hoots" by the owls, Angela was ready to reveal who was there.

"The owls have confirmed this is a friend of Knocker's and can be trusted. She is here in human form to seek your assistance." Angela paused a moment then continued, "They say they saw her come from the moon to help us!"

Remembering Ituria's Island was on the moon, Sara walked over to the small window in the kitchen and looked outside. It was a full moon tonight, just rising over the eastern sky, causing the leaves in the backyard to shimmer in the soft breeze.

"Okay!" Sara whispered with determination, more to herself than Angela. "Let's see what is needed and how we can help!"

Putting on her shoes, she walked to the back of the house and quietly unbolted the back door. Slipping through the door, she gently closed it so it would not make any noise that might wake up her father or brother. As she walked into the backyard toward the forest, she was constantly looking around; both for this friend of Knocker's, as well as for any poachers who might be out tonight. Commoners were not allowed out at night, not even in their own backyard! While the moonlight provided some light, it also cast eerie shadows in the night.

As she approached a tall tree, she heard rustling in the leaves on the ground behind it and stopped. "Who's there?" Sara whispered anxiously.

"Are you Sara?" a female voice asked.

"Yes, I am Sara," she replied.

"Are you Knocker's Sara?" the voice asked nervously, still unsure if she should show herself.

"Yes, I am Sara, friend of Knocker. Who are you?" Sara questioned, looking into the darkness, waiting for the owner of the voice to show herself, hoping the moonlight would reveal the visitor.

"I am Megan," came the cautious reply as a girl stepped out from behind the tree. "Knocker said I should contact you because I need your help."

Sara looked at the girl as she walked forward, the moonlight canceling out any colors, showing only shades of gray. Megan was not dressed like any of the local girls. Tall and slender, she was wearing a knee-length dress. Her long hair was braided and hanging down the left side almost to her waist, and she wore boots that came up to her knees. A satchel with a strap crossed over one shoulder and rested on her right side.

"Hi, Megan," Sara answered. "If Knocker sent you, then I will be glad to help."

"Thank you for your assistance, I will gratefully accept," Megan responded with relief as she bowed to Sara to show her respect. "We have learned a large cage of tiger cubs has been poached from this area, and they are being taken on a journey where they will ultimately die at the hand of humans for human profit." Pausing for a moment, she added calmly with resolve, "I am here to rescue them."

# Chapter Two

# MEGAN HAS A PLAN

"**W**hat have you learned, Megan, and how can I help?" Sara replied quietly, wanting to know more about the rescue attempt.

Walking closer to Sara, Megan answered, her voice low and composed, "Knocker and I have been listening to the poachers as they were making their plans. Knocker said he could not be here tonight because he has been seen by these poachers before, and his presence could jeopardize the mission, so he asked that I take his place."

Sara nodded as she remembered how Knocker confronted the poachers to protect her. They would recognize him if he appeared in the area since they were actively searching for him in the village.

Megan continued, "These tiger cubs were caught in the wild and will be taken to a tiger farm, raised until they are old enough to be killed, and their bodies sold as 'wild tiger' goods."

"Why?" Sara asked, confused by this revelation. "There are many tigers on the tiger farms; why do they have to steal these young cubs from the forest?"

"I overheard the poachers joking about it," Megan said, her voice becoming angry. "They said they could make more than double the money if they had 'wild' tigers—people want the 'wild' ones, even though there are so few wild tigers left…or maybe that's actually *why* they want them…because there are so few wild tigers. They made a deal with the tiger farmer—lots of money for wild tiger cubs!"

At this point, Sara could see Megan was becoming upset as she relayed what had been learned. Megan's eyes were wide with anger, her brows furrowed. Sara had to look twice at Megan's face; it looked like Megan's eyes had a red glow as she expressed her anger at this terrible arrangement.

"What can we do?" Sara asked quickly, deciding she must be seeing the moonlight reflecting in Megan's eyes. "How can we stop them? Is there a way to save these tiger cubs?"

Megan closed her eyes, refocusing on the mission at hand. Her voice became calm again, and the red glow was gone from her eyes when she reopened them. "Yes, I have a plan. The poachers will be passing through this area tonight, on the road in front of your house. Knocker advised me of your ability to assist him recently, and suggested I ask for your help."

Waving her hand and motioning for Sara to follow her, Megan turned and walked quietly toward the road, stopping behind a large tree that blocked them from view by anyone driving by.

"They will be here in a few minutes," Megan whispered as she looked around the tree. "I am going to stop them by putting a fallen tree across the road. During the time they are moving the tree, you and I will rescue the cubs. That is my plan." Reaching into her satchel, she added, "Look, I have these also."

Megan pulled out several pieces of cloth, about two feet by three feet in size. In the moonlight, the material had a grayish color with dark tiger-type stripes running through it. "We will make decoys of the cubs, so the poachers will not know when or where they were taken." Hesitating for a moment, Megan whispered worriedly, "Knocker has told me it is imperative that if you agree to help, I must make sure the poachers do not connect you with this rescue."

Sara nodded. "I understand. I'll be glad to help, just let me know how you want to get the cubs, and I'll do whatever is needed to rescue them! I promise I will stay hidden from the poachers and close to home so that I can get inside my house if they decide to check on my family."

"Thank you, Sara! Your safety must be my top priority!" Megan replied. "Let's go to where they will be stopped, and we can fill the cloth with leaves and fold them into squares. For each cub we rescue, we will put one of the decoys in its place. That way, the poachers will not know they are gone until they are long past this area."

"This sounds like a great plan!" Sara agreed. As she thought about the plan for a few moments, several questions came to mind. "Where should we wait for them? We will need to make the decoys as soon as possible, so they are ready when needed. And how will we get the cage opened?"

"We'll wait for them just around the bend in the road," Megan replied quickly to the first question, pointing in the direction of the curve in the road north of Sara's house. "That is where I will put the tree in the road. And don't worry about the cage," she added confidently, "I can handle that part."

Sara glanced quickly at Megan as she remembered Knocker was able to bend cage bars with his hands. She knew why Knocker was so strong, but could Megan be the same? She wanted to ask but wasn't sure if that was an appropriate question at this time. Should she wait? How would she even phrase it?

Seeing the questioning look in Sara's eyes, Megan replied calmly. "Yes, you are correct. I am the same type of being as Knocker, transformed to human form so that I will be able to blend in with the humans as I proceed with my plan."

Sara couldn't help but smile, this plan to rescue the cubs seemed to have a much greater chance of success with a dragon on the team!

"Thanks for letting me know!" Sara answered, realizing she could share her secret necklace and introduce Angela since Angela and Megan would be able to communicate with each other. She would not have let a human know of Angela's existence!

"Please allow me to introduce Angela. She will accompany us and will be of great assistance on your quest." Taking the tiger claw necklace out from underneath her shirt where it was hidden, Sara held it up for Megan to see as she continued. "Angela is the spirit of a tiger who was killed in these woods. She resides in this necklace, and she was the one who told me of your presence in the forest tonight. She can hear you and relay your messages to me when you are far away."

Looking at the necklace and bowing, Megan said, "Greetings, Angela, I am honored to meet you. Thank you for letting Sara know I was looking for her. Your help on this mission is also needed and greatly appreciated."

Speaking to Sara, Angela replied "Please tell Megan I will be glad to assist, and I will relay any messages needed to you if you and she are separated."

After Sara relayed the message, Megan nodded.

"Angela, I appreciate your help." Looking at Sara again, Megan said quietly, "One more thing before we start our mission. Sara, I need to give you this, just in case."

Looking down at a small vial as Megan handed it to her, Sara remembered back to when Knocker had given her a similar vial—containing an invisibility potion!

# Chapter Three

# TIME TO START THE MISSION

"Do I need to take this now?" Sara asked with hesitation, looking at Megan. The last time she took the potion, hearing her voice without being able to see her had frightened the cubs. "The cubs will be afraid of me if I am an invisible voice floating in the cage," she added. "Visible is better when trying to reach the cubs."

"No, you do not need to take this now," Megan answered quickly, wanting to reassure her. "This is for emergencies only. As I noted, you must not be seen under any circumstances."

"Okay, agreed. I will keep it in case of an emergency and if there is no alternative," Sara said as she nodded and slipped the vial into her pants pocket. Once the vial was secure, she asked, "Knocker had a translation stone that allowed me to talk with the cubs. Is that available?"

"Yes," Megan replied. "Let me give you the translation stone now. It is in this satchel in the inside pocket." Megan took off the satchel she had hanging over her shoulder.

"You keep the satchel with you. It should be big enough to carry the cubs; and the translation stone will be inside." Handing the large satchel over to Sara, she continued. "This way if we get separated, you can still talk with the cubs and get them to leave the cage. Here you go!"

After giving the bag to Sara, Megan continued. "You must keep the stone safe! It is the only one I have. If we get separated, I will communicate through Angela. One more thing; Knocker told me you know how to contact Guardian, is this correct?"

"That is right," Sara agreed as she put the satchel strap over her shoulder and held it tight. "If needed, I can call him for help. Last time, Guardian was able to transport us to Ituria's Island on the moon." Wondering how it would work on Megan's mission, she asked, "Will Guardian transport you also if I call out to him for help?" Sara didn't want to leave Megan alone or in danger while she was rescuing the cubs.

"No," Megan answered decisively. "I will stay until my mission is complete. If you are in danger, I will let you know through Angela to leave. If I say to leave, you must do so immediately!" Megan's voice was anxious again, knowing that she had to keep Sara safe.

"Understood, Megan, I will do as you say. Hopefully, that will not be necessary, but it is an option if needed." Sara said. "What's next?"

Turning toward the forest to the north and moving forward in the dark, Megan replied, "Time to start the mission! Follow me!"

Sara turned and followed quickly behind. Luckily, the moon was bright tonight; it would help them succeed on their mission!

Going north for several hundred yards until they reached the curve in the road, Sara saw a large tree lying along the side of the road. It looked over forty feet long and at least two feet in diameter on the large end.

Motioning to Sara to wait, Megan walked over to the tree, easily picked up one end, and quickly dragged it across the road, blocking the entire road. Sara watched as Megan effortlessly moved the giant tree. *Megan is a strong dragon indeed!* Now the truck would not be able to get through; the poachers would have to stop and deal with the tree blocking the road, and that is exactly what they needed.

"I left it on the side of the road in case someone else would be taking this road tonight." Megan whispered after she walked back to Sara. "We only want to stop the one truck. We don't need others to be stopped or to lend them assistance!"

"Agreed!" Sara replied. "Let's go ahead and fill the fabric up so we will be ready. How many cubs will we be rescuing? Will we need a decoy for each?"

"Yes, hopefully, we can make one for each," Megan said as she laid the first piece of fabric on the ground and started scooping leaves into the middle. "I have heard there are seven, barely able to walk, so we will need to be ready to assist them to escape."

Rumbling noises to the south warned of an approaching truck, causing both Sara and Megan to pause and look toward the sound, then turn quickly back to continue making the decoys.

"We must hurry!" Megan whispered. "We must be ready!" She folded up the first piece, moved it to the side, and took another piece of fabric, starting again.

Working quickly, the seven decoys were made and moved next to the road so they would be ready when needed.

"Sara," Megan whispered, "we will wait here until the truck stops. Then I will open the bars, and you can slip in to rescue the cubs!"

Crouching low to the ground, they waited. The rumbling sounds were getting louder, a large truck was making its way toward them. Hopefully, it was the one they were waiting for!

Rounding the corner, the headlights of the truck revealed the fallen tree in the road, and the sound of screeching brakes quickly followed. Stopping just before hitting the tree, the poachers got out and started yelling.

"What are we going to do now?" asked one with frustration.

"Let's go see if there is a way around it," replied the other as he pulled a flashlight out of the truck and started shining it on the tree.

The two men walked toward the tree and started discussing quietly how they would be able to get such a large tree out of the road.

Tapping Sara on the shoulder, Megan waved to Sara to follow her. They quickly made it to the back of the truck. It was an open-bed truck, no walls to worry about. There was a large metal cage in the center, and thrown over the cage was a tarp, covering most of the cage with only a few inches of the cage showing around the bottom.

"Sara," Megan whispered, "let's grab the decoys and get to the back of the truck. I'll get the cage bars open enough for you to slip in."

As the poachers stood talking next to the fallen tree, Megan and Sara carried the decoys and set them down near the truck. Megan then reached out and started pulling on the bars to make an opening big enough for Sara to slip through.

Disturbed by the activity, one of the cubs started to whimper, "I'm scared."

"Shhhh, little one, it's okay," Megan whispered to console it. "We are here to rescue you!"

# Chapter Four

# SARA IS TRAPPED!

O nce Megan bent the bars far enough for Sara to slip in, she motioned for Sara to come forward. "Sara, crawl in and hand out the cubs to me one at a time, and I'll hand one of the decoys back to you."

Moving quickly, Sara climbed onto the back of the truck, slipped into the cage, and kneeled next to the group of cubs. They started backing away from her and crying because they didn't know what was happening; they were scared.

Knowing she had the translation stone, Sara whispered to the young cubs. "Listen to me, we are here to rescue you, but you must be quiet. If they hear us, we might not make it."

"Okay," said one of the cubs softly. The others fell silent, waiting for Sara's next move.

"I'm going to pick you up and hand you to my friend Megan, one at a time," Sara whispered. "Megan will keep you safe! Please come to me so we can get you free!"

One of the cubs walked slowly over to her through the hay pile in the back of the cage. Picking it up gently, she turned and handed it to Megan, who gave her one of the fabric decoys to put in its place.

"Bury the decoy in the hay a little," Megan whispered, "so it will look like a sleeping tiger cub!"

Sara put the material decoy half buried in the hay and called for another cub. "Please come here, and you can be rescued!"

Another cub walked over to her and whispered, "Thank you. My little sister, Bonnie, is not able to walk, so you will need to help her."

"Let me get you out, and then I will look for her. I will make sure she is safe!" Sara whispered as she picked up the cub and handed it to Megan. Taking another decoy, she placed it in the hay also, so it looked like a sleeping cub. Then she moved over to find the sick one so that she could rescue it also. "Where are you, Bonnie?" Sara whispered. "If you can't move, please give me a soft call, and I will come to you! We will rescue all of you!"

From in front of the truck came a loud call from one of the poachers. "Let's use the truck to move the tree; that's the easiest way!"

"Okay, Doug, how do we do that?" came the reply.

"There's a rope in the back by the cage," Doug yelled. "Here's the flashlight. Get it, and we'll tie it to the front of the truck!"

Megan disappeared from Sara's view, and Angela called to Sara, "Megan says take the invisibility potion now!"

Reaching into her pocket, Sara grabbed the vial with the potion. Remembering Knocker's instructions from her previous rescue, she knew half of the vial was the correct amount for her size. She quickly opened the vial and swallowed half the contents, closed the vial, and put it back in her pocket. Staying motionless in the cage, she hoped the potion would work before the poacher came back to look for the rope.

She heard noises and felt the cage shake as someone jumped onto the back of the truck, and there were footsteps just outside the cage. "Where is it, Doug?" Tony asked.

"Tony, it should be over behind the cage, a big, coiled rope!" Doug replied. "I tied it to the floor with a chain."

Light from the flashlight flickered around the cage but didn't shine through the giant canvas covering it. "Got it!" Tony shouted as Sara heard the rattling of a chain to untie the rope. Then, there was a loud thud as Tony landed on the ground after jumping off the back of the truck, and the cage shook again from the shifting weight.

After hearing Tony running away from the truck, Sara whispered, "Little ones, we will still rescue you, I am still here."

"Doug," Tony yelled, "the rope is tied to the tree and the front bumper of the truck! Go ahead and back up. I'll let you know when the road is clear enough to pass."

Hearing the truck engine start up, Sara sat down closer to the remaining cubs, calling softly to them. "Don't worry little ones," she reassured, "I am still here. You will be okay; we just need to wait until my friend gets back!" While trying to keep her voice calm for the cubs, Sara was very worried about this turn of events, trying to figure out what Megan would do now, and how would they complete their mission?

A loud roar echoed through the forest! Tony waved frantically for Doug to get out of the truck! After Doug turned off the engine, Tony shouted, "Doug, I heard a tiger roar! Let's get it!"

"Yep," Doug agreed. "Let me grab my gun from the truck!"

As the two poachers ran into the forest, Angela spoke to Sara. "Sara, the roar was Megan. She says she is taking the two cubs to Ituria and will be back shortly!"

Another roar and a flash of blue light let Sara know that Megan had left for the moon with the first two cubs. Now, she was all alone inside a cage with five small tiger cubs. At least she was invisible!

# Chapter Five

# BACK ON THE ROAD

S itting in the cage with the cubs, she said softly, "My friend is taking the first two cubs to a safe place and will be back shortly. No need to worry, we will get you all to a safe place!"

"Where are you?" one called out. "I can't see you anymore."

"My friend used her magic to make me invisible so the poachers can't see me. I will stay with you until you are all safe!" Sara replied, remembering she was only a voice to them now. "Why don't we all get ready to leave now so we can all leave at once when my friend gets back? I have a large satchel here that I can carry you in, and we can all leave at one time."

"That sounds good, I don't want to be here!" said one of the cubs.

"Bonnie," Sara whispered, "please let me know where you are. I can come to pick you up. Your brother said you might need a little help."

"I'm over here," said a weak voice a little further away from the other cubs. "I can't move well. Please help me to get away!"

Crawling on her hands and knees over to the voice, Sara replied. "I am here now. You won't be able to see me, but I can see you and will pick you up and hold you in my arms while the others crawl into the bag."

First laying out the satchel so the other cubs could climb in, Sara reached out and gently picked up Bonnie, who was a tiny cub, smaller than the others. "Hi Bonnie, you are safe with me! If the rest of you can, please get into the bag so I can pick it up and leave as soon as we hear back that it is safe!"

Sounds from outside required an immediate change in plans! The poachers were coming back to the truck!

"I don't know how it got away! It sounded so close!" Tony called to Doug as they walked toward the truck.

"I believe you, man," Doug replied. "But we don't have time to be chasing tigers with this load, I have to get it delivered by morning. Let's get going!"

"Okay, Doug, let's get the tree moved and get out of here," Tony said. "I'll wave when the tree is out of the road. Keep backing up until you see my signal!"

The truck door opened and then slammed shut, and the engine started again. As the truck backed up, pulling the tree off the road, Sara realized that they needed to give the appearance of tiger cubs in the cage in case the poachers checked before continuing down the road.

"Everyone, back to where you were sleeping!" she whispered urgently. "Bonnie, I will hold onto you, and you will be invisible like me."

"Thank you!" Bonnie said, glad someone was taking care of her.

The cubs scampered out of the satchel and went back to their places in the hay. Sara checked the two decoys, making sure they were partially covered and looked like sleeping tiger cubs. Then she went over to a corner of the cage with Bonnie, holding her close so she was invisible.

The satchel! Reaching over, she quickly grabbed the satchel from the hay, putting it over her shoulder and holding it close so it would be invisible too! It had to look the same— just cubs sleeping in the hay!

"Doug, the tree is out of the way!" Tony shouted. "Let's get the chain off and we can be on our way!"

"Everyone, we must be quiet!" Sara whispered. "Remember you are sleeping!"

Footsteps approaching the back of the truck, and a chain rattling let Sara know Tony was putting the rope back next to the cage.

"Tony, while you're back there, make sure those cubs are okay. They are worth a lot of money!" Doug called out to him.

"Got it!" Tony answered. He lifted the side of the tarp and the light from a flashlight darted around on the hay, stopping here and there as it found several of the cubs in the hay, along with one of the decoys. Then the light went away, the tarp fell back down, and there were sounds of footsteps heading to the front of the truck.

"Looks like everyone is sleeping back there," Tony said to Doug. "Let's be on our way!"

"Good! Climb on in, we have a way to go before dawn. I'm anxious to turn these cubs over and get paid," Doug replied, ready to get this trip finished.

The cage started shaking as the truck began moving down the road again.

"What will happen now?" Bonnie asked. "How will your friend find you if we are not where she left you?"

"Do not worry, little one," Sara said, trying to comfort her. "My friend will find us; she is very talented. We just need to wait for her!"

But to Sara, the real question was even more worrisome—*How will Megan find us in a moving truck?*

Angela sensed Sara's worry and responded. "Don't worry, Sara, Megan will find you. I will let her know where we are as soon as she returns."

*We are a team!* Sara's courage was restored as she realized that she, Angela, and Megan could complete the mission and save the cubs as long as they worked together. She relaxed just a little, knowing that Angela was also looking out for them and could hear when Megan returned. Now all they could do was wait!

# *Chapter Six*

# ANOTHER TREE DOWN

The truck rumbled and creaked loudly as it traveled over the bumpy dirt road, bouncing Sara and the cubs about. They waited nervously for Megan's return, afraid to make a sound.

After several minutes in worried silence, Angela spoke to Sara. "Sara, Megan has returned. She will knock down another tree and put it in the road ahead of the truck. When the truck stops again, you must be ready to leave immediately. She will place the decoys next to the truck once it is stopped." Since only Sara could hear Angela, Sara needed to let the cubs know what was going on and get them ready!

"Listen little ones," she called to them, just loud enough over the rumble of the truck so they could hear her. "My friend is returning. She says as soon as the truck stops, we need to get out of the truck and hide in the woods."

"Hi, this is Henry," one of the cubs replied. "Should we get back in your carrier?"

"Hi, Henry, I'm Sara. Yes, we need to do that now!" Sara responded. Crawling over to where the cubs were lying down, she spread out the satchel again so that they could crawl in. "Bonnie, you will stay with me. The rest of you, please get back into the satchel so I can just grab it and go as soon as the truck stops."

"Okay!" replied another. "I'm Nathan, I'm getting into your carrier now. Come on everyone! Let's get ready to escape!" He was doing his best to be brave for the other cubs; however, Sara could hear the nervousness in his voice.

"Thank you, Nathan!" she replied. "I'll let you make sure everyone is ready! Let me know when everyone is in the carrier and ready to go."

"Yes, I will help!" Nathan said with determination. "Let's go! Henry, Jacob, and Martha, let's get into Sara's carrier so she can take us out of this cage."

"Thanks, Nathan," Sara replied gratefully. "I really appreciate your help!"

Sounds of little creatures moving through the hay told Sara the tiger cubs were on their way to the satchel. Hopefully, they would be ready to go when the truck stopped.

"Ready now, Sara!" Nathan called out after a few minutes.

And just in time! The truck screeched to a halt as it stopped to avoid another tree across the road.

Doug jumped out of the truck and started yelling at someone. "What are you doing here? Did you do this? Get back here little girl. I'm talking to you!"

Jumping out of the truck after Doug, Tony called to him. "What did you see? I thought I saw a girl standing in front of the tree!"

"I did too!" Doug agreed. "But then she disappeared! Which way did she go? Did you see?"

"No," Tony replied. "She was there, and then she was gone! What should we do?"

"Sara," Angela called to her, getting her attention away from the poachers' discussion. "Megan is here and will distract the poachers. It is time to go. The decoys are just outside the truck."

Sara didn't need to be told twice! Sara grabbed the satchel with her free hand and put it over her shoulder. Holding Bonnie carefully in her other hand, she went through the bent bars. Looking around quickly, she could see the decoys lying near a tree, so she climbed off the truck and ran over to them.

"Listen, buddies," Sara whispered, "I am going to put the satchel down so I can pick up the decoys and put them in the cage. I will be right back."

Sara set the satchel down gently so the cubs would be safe. She set Bonnie down in the satchel and whispered, "Nathan, please watch Bonnie for a few moments. I will be right back."

Grabbing the decoys, Sara quickly placed them through the cage bars in various places on the hay and threw a little more hay on top. She needed to make it look like little cubs sleeping in the hay! Then she raced back to the tree to pick up Bonnie so she was secure and invisible.

The truck's engine stopped, and the poachers were out in front of it yelling again. Sara and the cubs needed to disappear! Picking up the satchel and holding it close, it too became invisible. Now they needed to hide in the woods close by so that Megan could find them!

"Everyone, you must be very quiet," whispered Sara as she walked away carefully from the truck, looking to make sure she didn't step on any sticks or make any noise. Since they were invisible, only noise would reveal them to the poachers.

Walking into the woods where she could no longer see the truck, Sara sat down next to a large tree, still holding Bonnie and the satchel close.

"Okay, let's stay as still as possible until Megan comes back for us!" Sara said softly. "She will be back soon, I am sure!"

"Megan will return soon," Angela confirmed. "She will find you, so please stay where you are safe!"

"Thanks, Angela," Sara whispered, "I will wait until you hear from Megan again."

Sara and the cubs sat in silence, hoping the poachers would leave. She could hear them searching for Megan.

"Where did she go?" Tony shouted. "She was just beyond the tree. Do you think she had something to do with the tree being down?"

"She is just a puny girl," Doug replied with a nasty tone. "But she may have some friends out here—maybe she is connected to that boy we are looking for!"

"Do you think so?" Tony asked.

"Yes, I wouldn't put it past that boy to be chopping down trees." Doug went to the truck and opened the door. "I'm getting my gun and maybe we can find them both!" he shouted. "Let's go!"

Sara's mind was racing. Doug was still looking for Knocker and thinks he is connected to Megan! Doug may not realize how close he was to being right. But for now, Sara's main concern was the safety of these small cubs. Hugging them even closer, she knew she had to be courageous to protect them as she was their only hope!

# Chapter Seven

# RACE THROUGH THE WOODS

Footsteps were running through the woods, branches snapping and leaves crunching. Whomever it was, they weren't worried if they were heard or not. The sounds were getting closer, causing Sara to catch her breath. *Who could it be? Megan, or the poachers?*

The footsteps stopped at the front of the truck; it was Doug and Tony, returning from their search for Megan.

"Did you see where she went?" Doug asked, standing in the light from the headlights of the truck. "I thought I saw her run to the north, but I didn't see anything. Does that sound right? Which way should we be looking?"

"I don't know," Tony answered. "Maybe we just get the tree moved and get out of here. Two downed trees on the same road on the same night? Things are getting a little weird—especially that girl popping in and out. I've never seen her around here before, and she was sure dressed different from the locals."

"You know, Tony, you're right!" Doug exclaimed. "That boy was dressed differently too. I bet they really are working together! Maybe we should go back into the woods to look for them? I bet they are waiting for us close to the other side of this tree."

"No, Doug," Tony argued. "If they are waiting for us, then they have the upper hand, and there may be more of them. Let's get out of here while we can. We can always come back later and find them when we have more men with us."

"Okay," Doug replied gruffly. "For now, I agree with you, we need to leave before they gang up on us. But I'm not going to stop looking for them, no way! Someone in this area knows who they are and I'm not going to stop until I find out!"

"Doug, look over here," Tony called out as his flashlight lit up the end of the tree. "We can probably get the truck through here—maybe use the truck to push the tree a little bit. That would be the quickest way." Tony was walking around in front of the tree, trying to figure out how to get them back on track.

"Okay," Doug said as he climbed back into the truck. "I'm going to push the tree, and you watch it. Let me know when we are clear!"

"Will do!" Tony agreed.

The truck engine started again, and Sara could hear it backing up and pushing forward, trying to move the tree enough for the truck to get past.

"Sara," Angela called to her. "There is a presence here, I sense another tiger nearby. Please be careful! I will reach out to see if I can determine who it is and if they are friend or foe!"

Crouching lower to the ground even though she was invisible, Sara realized that things were getting a little complicated, questions racing through her mind. *Is Megan safe from the poachers? Will she be here to protect us if the tiger attacks us, not knowing we were trying to help? How will I get back home?*

Seeking Angela's calmness, Sara whispered, "Angela, what should I do?"

"Sara, be calm. Megan is safe." Angela's voice echoed through Sara's mind. *Thank goodness, Megan is safe!*

"Sara," Angela called to her. "Megan is going to stay by the poachers to keep them from finding you. You must start heading south. Follow the road. If you are still invisible, you can walk on the road. But you must not make any noises that will reveal your presence!"

"Agreed," Sara replied. "Please tell Megan we will get on the road and start following it back to my house. I am still invisible, so we will not be seen."

Quietly standing up and holding Bonnie and the satchel close to her, she started walking slowly toward the road. As long as she held the cubs close, they were invisible. She just had to be brave and get to the road and head back to her house.

"Let Megan know I am on my way," Sara whispered softly to Angela. Then to the cubs, "Little ones, we are on our way! Please be quiet; we are invisible but can be heard!"

"Yes, Sara," whispered Nathan. "We understand!"

Sara worked her way behind the truck once it had stopped moving back and forth pushing the tree. She could hear them talking as she made it to the road, and she hoped that she was not making any noise!

"Okay, Tony, ready to go!" Doug yelled over the engine. "Check on those cubs one more time, and we'll be on our way!"

"Got it, Doug!" Tony called back.

As Sara started walking down the road, she looked back at the truck. Tony had his flashlight and was shining it in the cage. She started walking faster, they had to get away now!

A few moments later, Tony yelled, "Doug, they're gone! They're gone!"

"What do you mean they're gone?" Doug screamed as he jumped out of the truck and headed to the cage.

"Look!" Tony screamed back and pulled out a piece of material, the leaves falling out as he picked it up. "The bars are bent, just like last time. Someone stole the cubs! And someone put pieces of material in here to make it look like there were still cubs here! It must have something to do with that girl and the boy we saw last time!"

"We are going to check every house on this road until we find that girl!" Doug yelled. "She isn't getting away with my cubs! She'll know where the boy is too!"

"Let's look here first to see if there are any clues!" Tony said. "Maybe we can find out when they were taken and who may have taken them."

Tony climbed onto the truck and pulled off the tarp. "Look here Doug, someone put a bunch of decoys in back. There's no way to know when they were taken!"

"I know it was after the last town," Doug replied angrily. "I saw them moving myself back then. They weren't decoys. So, it's between there and here, and we're going to go into every house on the way until find them!"

# Chapter Eight

# ANOTHER TIGER!

Sara heard the truck behind her, and it was coming up fast! She jumped off the road and let it pass by. She saw the truck stop up the road next to a small house, and the two men jumped out and ran to the front door. Pounding on the door, they screamed to the residents to open the door and let them in.

Hurrying past the house, Sara knew she needed to beat the poachers to her house, but how?

"Angela, please tell Megan I need to make it home before the poachers!" Sara said urgently.

After a few moments, Angela replied, "Yes, Sara, I have done so. Megan understands, and she is heading back your way. You have another visitor, though, who is just ahead of you. The tiger can smell us and is heading in our direction."

"It can smell us?" Sara whispered in a panic. "What can I do? I can't outrun a tiger!"

"Calm, Sara, you do not need to outrun it. Find a spot among the trees and sit down," Angela responded calmly. "You do not need to run from

this tiger. She does not seek to harm you. She is looking for something and thinks you may be able to help her."

"Are you sure?" Sara asked.

"Yes, Sara, this tiger has told me it means you no harm," Angela answered.

"Okay," Sara replied. "I'm heading back into the woods now."

Turning back into the wooded area, Sara sat down on the ground next to a large tree. She held Bonnie close and hugged the satchel so that they would all remain invisible.

"Sara, the tiger is close now," Angela said. "You have your translation stone; call out to it—tell it you are a friend of tigers."

"Tiger," Sara started, not really knowing what to say. "I am a friend of tigers and on a mission to rescue tiger cubs."

From the darkness came a low growl, and then a large tiger appeared in the moonlight. Much larger than Sara had imagined, this full-grown tiger stood taller than she was as she sat under the tree. It was looking around and sniffing intently, trying to find her.

"I am here, but I am invisible," Sara tried to explain. "Please let me know how I can help you."

The tiger sniffed as it got closer to Sara but did not make a sound. While its eyes could not see her, it could smell her and focused in on her location. When it was within inches of her, it asked warily, "Why do you smell of tiger? Where are the tiger cubs you say you are rescuing?"

Moving her hand away from her body, Bonnie became visible and seemed to be floating in the air. "Here is one of the cubs, her name is Bonnie," Sara answered. "I rescued her and four others; the others are in my bag."

The satchel became visible as she moved it away from her body and placed it on the ground in front of her. "Here are the other cubs," Sara said softly. "We have rescued them from a cage and are trying to escape from the poachers who stole them."

Although Bonnie appeared asleep in Sara's hands, after a few seconds near the tiger, she sniffed a little, opened her eyes and looked up at the tiger, then cried out, "Mama!"

"Bonnie, my little one, are you okay?" the tiger replied lovingly as she rubbed noses with Bonnie. "Do you know where your brothers are?"

"I'm down here, Mama!" called Henry as he ran over to be with them.

The large tiger crouched down and gathered her two cubs to her, licking them with her tongue and nuzzling them with her nose. "I am so glad I found you!" Looking into the satchel, she asked, "Where is Justin?"

"Justin was rescued before us and was taken to a safe place," Henry said as he cuddled up with his mother. "These creatures saved us from a human's cage."

Looking up to the space where Sara was, the tiger continued, "Thank you for rescuing my children. I was chasing some humans away from my den, and when I returned, my cubs were missing; I have been looking for them ever since. Where has Justin been taken?"

"He was rescued by my friend Megan and taken to Ituria's Island," Sara replied. "Animals are safe from humans on Ituria's Island."

"Please tell your friend I need to get my son Justin back. We need to be a family again!" the tiger said urgently, wanting to get her missing son back with her other two cubs.

"Please know that we will get your family together again soon," Sara said, then her voice turned anxious as she described her current dilemma. "My problem now is that I need to get to my house before these humans find out I have helped the cubs. If they find out I am out tonight and connected to the cubs, my whole family will be in danger. These humans are just as cruel to humans as they are to animals!"

"Thank you for rescuing my children," the tiger said in Sara's general direction. "My name is Katrina. Please let me know what I can do to help you get home. How will your invisibility work when you return to your home? Can you turn visible again so these humans can see you are there and won't hurt your family?"

"I have a short period of time left where I will still be invisible, and then the magic will wear off, and I will be visible…" Sara started, stopping in mid-sentence as they both heard noises indicating someone, or something, was heading their way.

The sound of footsteps rapidly approaching through the bushes silenced everyone as they all turned nervously in the direction to see if they could determine who was running in their direction. Seeing the cubs vulnerable on the ground, Sara quickly picked up Bonnie and the satchel, making them invisible again, and at the same time whispering, "Hide!" to the tiger.

The tiger nodded and instantly blended into the shadows and underbrush, waiting for this new visitor, anxiously wondering if they had been found by the poachers.

# Chapter Nine

# MEGAN RETURNS

"**G**reetings, Sara," Megan said as she took a long breath upon entering the small opening in the woods where Sara had stopped, and she talked in the direction she sensed Sara was sitting. "I have put a hole in one of the tires of the humans' truck, so it will take them a while to fix it."

Turning to the tiger who was hidden in the underbrush, Megan bowed and said respectfully, "Greetings, Katrina. I am Megan. I am helping Sara rescue these tiger cubs. Can I please ask for your assistance to keep these cubs safe while I get Sara back to her home? I must get her home before the humans get there. I can then come back here and take you and the cubs to a safe place."

"Greetings, Megan," Katrina replied as she walked into the clearing, bowing back to Megan. "Sara has indicated that you have rescued my Justin and have taken him to this safe place, and you also assisted in rescuing these other five cubs, including my two young ones, Bonnie and Henry. I will be glad to watch over them while you return Sara to her home, and then we can go get my Justin back."

"Thank you, Katrina, your help is greatly appreciated," Megan said. "I promise that you will be reunited with your Justin."

"Sara," Megan continued, turning to where Sara was sitting, still invisible, "the only way to get you home before the humans is to fly. I will change into my natural form, and then have you climb on my back, and we can beat them to your house."

"That sounds like it will work," Sara agreed.

"Let's get Katrina and the cubs in a safe place, and then we will be on our way," Megan added. "I saw a small cave as I was running here, and it might be a good hiding spot. Follow me!"

Passing the first fallen tree that had been moved out of the road by the poachers, Megan led the group to a small opening in the rocks, just big enough for Katrina to slip in. After Katrina had settled inside, Sara put Bonnie next to her, and then the other four cubs, keeping the satchel with her.

"Megan, the satchel has the translation stone," Sara stated. "I will need to keep that with me if I am going to communicate with Katrina and the cubs, as well as with you."

"Agreed, Sara," Megan replied. "Katrina, are you and the cubs good until I return?"

"Yes, Megan, we should be safe here," Katrina responded. "Once you are gone, we will move further back in the cave and keep silent so only you will know we are here."

"Thank you again for your assistance, Katrina," Megan said with appreciation. "I must keep Sara safe from these humans. If they knew she was helping us, they would punish her and her family!"

"I understand," Katrina replied sadly. "These humans are dangerous to humans and creatures alike. Please continue your mission!"

"Thank you, Katrina! Please be safe!" Sara said. She watched as Katrina backed further into the cave, gently picking up Bonnie with her mouth. The other four cubs waddled back into the darkness.

When they could not be seen from the entrance, Megan turned and started walking toward a larger opening among the trees. "Sara, I need a bit of room, so please stay where you are."

"Okay, Megan," Sara replied, not quite knowing what to expect.

Sara watched in awe as Megan closed her eyes for just a moment and transformed into a fantastically large, ruby-scaled dragon, standing twice as tall as Sara and almost 20 feet long, her ruby scales shimmering in the moonlight. Her large gray wings extended toward the highest branches of the tree.

Megan's eyes glowed red in the darkness, and as she turned her head to look at Sara, the moonlight reflected on her face, showing her sharp dragon teeth and giving her a ferocious look. *She's a large dragon indeed! So glad she's a friend!*

"Wow, Megan," Sara exclaimed, "you are a beautiful dragon!"

"Thank you for your kind words, Sara," Megan replied in Sara's general direction. "Now we must get you home before the poachers get there. And hopefully, you will turn visible again soon!"

"What should I do?" Sara asked. She wasn't sure how she was supposed to get on Megan's back or what to hold onto if Megan took off into the air.

"You will need to climb onto my back near my wings," Megan replied. "Then hold onto one of the spikes on my back so you don't fall when I take off."

"Okay, Megan," Sara answered. "Here I go!"

Gently climbing onto Megan's back, Sara settled in between one of the wings and back and grabbed onto one of the many spikes lining Megan's back from her head to her tail. Putting the satchel over her shoulder so it wouldn't fall off, she held on tight.

"I'm ready now!" Sara called to her.

"Hold on!" Megan replied. "I will have to go straight up to get out of the trees!"

Megan jumped into the air and with one flap of her wings, she was propelled up and out of the forest into the night sky above. Sara was hanging on tight, so she didn't fall backward onto the ground. After leveling off, Megan headed south.

"I will follow the road, and we should be at your house in just a few minutes," Megan said.

"What a different view from up in the air!" Sara exclaimed as she saw the moonlight shining on the trees below. "It's so beautiful up here!"

"Yes, the forest is a beautiful place, I agree!" Megan replied. "Okay, there is your house now. Hold on! We're going in fast, so we aren't seen!"

As Megan dived into the forest below, Sara hugged Megan's back and closed her eyes, this was a bit too scary! She hoped Megan wasn't going to crash into the trees.

# Chapter Ten

# Home before the Poachers

"**I**t's okay now, Sara," Megan called to Sara softly as she was clinging tightly to Megan. "We've landed."

Sara opened her eyes and loosened her grip on Megan's back.

"Oh, great!" Sara replied with a sigh of relief. "It was a little scary coming down so quickly."

"No worries. I would not have let you fall," Megan said confidently. "Give me a moment to change back into human form. Being a dragon might cause a lot of unwelcome attention."

Megan closed her eyes. This time, it took over a minute for her to transform back into the human girl Sara had seen before. "It is very hard to transform back into such a small form. It's a good thing my strength does not leave me when I am this small!"

"I agree," Sara replied. "It is amazing to me how you can move those heavy trees!"

Megan smiled for just a moment, and then her voice turned serious. "Sara, listen to me. You must go home now, while you are invisible. Hide in your room until you are visible again, okay?"

"Yes, I will," Sara agreed.

"Have Angela tell me when you are visible again," Megan continued. "I will keep the humans away from your house until I get the message. Also, I need to get the satchel with the translation stone again. You can have Angela help talk with the tigers and cubs; however, if I need to talk to the humans, I will need the translation stone."

"Agreed. That sounds like the best approach," Sara responded as she took the satchel off her shoulder and handed it to Megan. As she held it out it became visible again, floating in the air, and Megan took it from Sara and put it over her shoulder.

"Take care, Sara," Megan said. "Once you are safe, I will get Katrina and the cubs out of here."

"I'm going inside now," Sara answered softly. "I will let Angela tell you as soon as I am visible again so you can continue your mission. Thank you, Megan!"

The moonlight lit the backyard enough for Sara to run to the back door of her house and she went inside. Being invisible, she just needed to go in quietly, she didn't want to wake her father and brother up. Slipping into her room, she locked the door and put the chair in front, like she did last time she was invisible. Her last line of defense to keep anyone from learning her secret!

It was about 20 minutes later when she heard the truck coming down the road. The brakes screeched as the truck stopped, and she heard the truck doors slamming. She was still invisible! She should change any minute, though, and she just wished it would happen already! Going over to her dresser, she reached for her nightgown. She wanted to be ready to put it on as soon as she became visible, so she could look like she had been sleeping. As she held up the nightgown, she could see her hands again!

"Angela, tell Megan I'm visible again," Sara whispered urgently. "She does not need to deal with the poachers now!"

"Yes, Sara, I will do so!" Angela replied.

Slipping into her nightgown and taking off her shoes, Sara removed the chair and opened the lock on the bedroom door. Then she went to lie in her bed, rumpling up the covers like she had been sleeping for a while. She closed her eyes so she would look like she was sleeping if her father came to check on her. However, she listened anxiously to see what would happen next, knowing that the poachers would be pounding on the door at any moment!

A loud knocking on the door was followed by Doug yelling, "Let me in, I need to see who lives here!"

Sara's father woke up and called back as he got to the front room, "We are all sleeping here. No one has gone outside. What is the matter?"

"Some girl was wandering around the woods tonight, and I know there is a girl who lives here. I need to see her, now!" Doug yelled back.

Running back and peeking into Sara's room, her father saw Sara in bed, and she looked like she was sleeping.

"She's sleeping. She hasn't left the house!" he answered after returning to the front of the house.

"Let me in, and I'll see for myself! I need to know if she is the girl I saw in the woods tonight!" Doug screamed through the door.

"Okay, okay!" her father replied as he opened the door. "Let me go wake her up, if you haven't woken her up already by your yelling."

Sara got out of bed, ran her fingers through her hair to mess it up a little bit to look like she just woke up, and headed out her bedroom door to the front room.

"What's going on?" she asked slowly, pretending to be half asleep.

"Sara, this man says he saw a girl running around in the woods tonight. He wants to make sure it wasn't you." Her father was very nervous and was trying to explain why there was a strange man in the house so late at night.

"Did you leave this house tonight, girl?" Doug yelled at her.

"No, I've been sleeping. What happened?" Sara said, trying to sound confused. She needed to make sure Doug did not suspect her of going outside, as her whole family would be punished if he did.

"None of your business what happened!" Doug answered gruffly. "Have you seen any new girls in the village or at the market? Someone with long hair?"

"No, I haven't seen anyone new. I only go to the market to get a few things then come right home," she responded. "There have been no new people at the market that I have seen. What is going on?"

"Listen, some new girl is in this area tonight. She stole something from me, and I'm going to find her. I'm not leaving until I do!" Doug was furious. "Don't anyone in this house go outside tonight, understand! I'm going to see if there is anything where the first tree fell into the road. Maybe there is a clue to who did it!" Stomping out of the house, he slammed the door behind him.

*Chapter Eleven*

# WAITING TO
# BE RESCUED

**"S**ara, are you okay?" her father asked, still shaken by this latest intrusion. "He's gone now, so you should be safe now. Let's try to get back to sleep."

"Thanks," Sara replied. "What could he have been talking about? Do you know?"

"Ever since someone stole his tiger cubs a few weeks ago, he has been scouring this area, looking for a boy. Now he says there is a girl, too!" The father shook his head. "I wish they would just leave us alone!"

"I know, Father," Sara said, trying to calm him down. "I feel the same way. I agree, we need to try and get some sleep, you have a busy day at work tomorrow!"

"Agreed." He replied. "We will be off at dawn. Please stay in the house tomorrow. Who knows

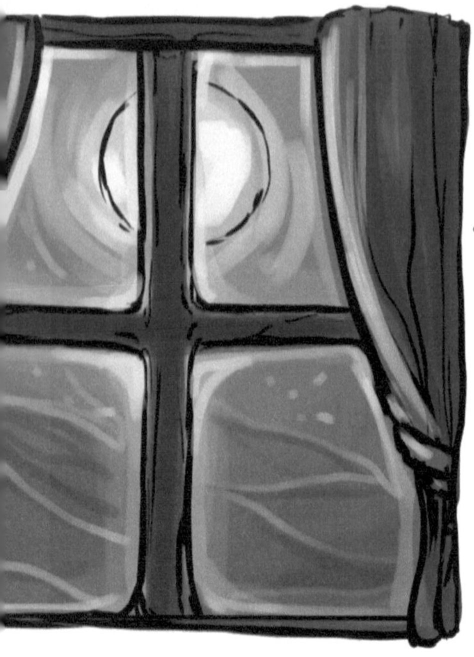

what will happen at the marketplace after tonight's visit."

"I will stay home, I promise," Sara said softly. "Let's just try to go back to sleep!"

Heading to their separate rooms, Sara got to her bedroom and closed the door.

"Angela!" Sara whispered. "What is happening? Is Megan okay? Are the tiger and cubs okay? Something must be going on out there."

"Caution is needed," Angela said in Sara's mind. "One of the humans is still outside this house. You must not take any action at this time."

*They didn't both leave!* Sara climbed into bed, waiting for updates from Angela.

"You must let Megan know the humans have separated. She must watch for both of them!" She whispered to Angela. "Is Katrina still hidden with the cubs?"

"Oh no!" Sara gasped as she realized that the tiger and cubs were hiding right next to where the first tree was lying. "Katrina and the cubs need to know that one of the humans is heading right for them. Please tell her to back up in the cave as far as she can and let her know Megan is also heading her way!"

"It is done," Angela replied a few moments later. "Megan and Katrina will wait until these humans have gone."

Now all they could do was wait for the poachers to leave the area, so Megan could get the tigers out into the open and transport them to the moon. How long would that be? Sara was worried since it did not appear that Doug was going to leave any time soon!

"Sara, Megan is calling to me!" Angela said.

Sara could hear what sounded like a large animal growling in the woods. That must be Megan's natural voice without the translation stone!

"Megan is waiting at the first tree." Angela continued. "She says the poacher is calling out and getting close to Katrina and the cubs. She will lead him away, and you must leave and get Katrina and the cubs to the moon."

"What?" Sara asked. "Megan should not reveal herself to the poachers, tell her, please! We can wait until they leave!"

"Megan says she can wait no longer. She will not let the human get near the tiger and cubs." Angela relayed the information as she was receiving it. "It is up to you to rescue them now!"

Quickly changing out of her nightgown into her day clothes, she slipped on her shoes and snuck out the back door again. She could hear yelling in the distance in the direction where Katrina was hiding.

"Tony, I see her!" Doug yelled back to the house. "Come over now! Hurry!"

Hearing footsteps behind her, Sara hid in the bushes. She watched as Tony ran past her toward Doug's voice.

"I got you now, little girl!" Doug screamed into the darkness. "You won't get away from me this time!"

# Chapter Twelve

## TRIP TO THE MOON

"Sara be calm," Angela said to Sara. "Katrina and the cubs have not been found. Megan has gotten the humans to follow her. We must move quickly though."

"Agreed." Sara whispered. "Please let me know what you hear from the creatures in the forest. Is it safe to go to Katrina now?"

"Wait one more moment until they are far enough away that they will not hear us," Angela responded.

Sara crouched down and waited for Angela to tell her it was okay to go to the cave. She could still hear Doug shouting in the distance, and he didn't sound happy. "We must go soon before they return!" Sara whispered.

"Yes," Angela replied. "Now is the time. Stay low and do not make any of the branches or trees move. Katrina awaits you at the cave."

Sara realized she did not have the satchel any-more, how were they going to get the cubs to the moon? There had to be a way to get them all together, she just needed to figure it out!

As she crept toward the cave, she realized that she could roll her shirt up a bit to her waist, and it would make a small pocket to hold the cubs. She would still hold Bonnie since she was so fragile, but the others should be okay.

Kneeling in front of the cave, she waved for Katrina and the cubs to come to her. "Angela," Sara whispered, "tell them I need them to come out now. We need to leave as soon as possible!"

"I have relayed your message and Katrina understands," Angela responded after a few moments. "She will hand you Bonnie. She asks how you will hold the others?"

"Look," Sara explained. "I will roll my shirt up to form a pocket, and they can stay there. Please tell her we all need to be together when I call Guardian. We must be holding the cubs or they may get left behind!"

Katrina's head appeared at the entrance to the cave, and she was holding Bonnie. Sara gently took Bonnie in one hand and held the pocket she had made in her shirt with the other so that Katrina could put the others there. Okay, all four cubs were in the pocket. What's next?

Sara scooted back and then stood up. Turning to the open area Megan used to transform into a dragon, she hoped Katrina would follow. "Angela, please tell Katrina to get right next to me. Put her shoulder next to my leg, we need to be touching so she doesn't get left here."

"She understands and is on her way. You must hurry, the humans have lost Megan and they are on their way back now!" Angela called to Sara.

Katrina started growling softly, looking at Sara. Sara didn't have the translation stone so could not understand her.

"Sara, Katrina indicates you should take the cubs back first. She will stand guard so the humans cannot get to you or the cubs," Angela relayed to Sara. "Then she will find and fight with Megan. You must leave now!"

Looking up to the sky, Sara shouted, "Guardian, I need your help now!"

As Sara watched the blue beam quickly approaching from the moon to carry her away, she hoped that Katrina would be safe staying here with the poachers heading to this spot. "Angela, please let Megan know that Katrina is staying to help!"

"I have done so!" Angela said.

Within seconds the blue beam landed on Sara, and she was pulled quickly up into the sky. Although she tried to stay awake, she felt dizzy and as she lost consciousness, she knew she was on her way to the moon.

"Sara!" said a voice, calling for her to wake up. "Sara, you must wake up!"

"Where am I," Sara said slowly, trying to wake up. "Did we make it?"

"Yes, Sara, this is Ituria," said the voice. As Sara opened her eyes, she saw the large unicorn leaning down with a concerned look. "We will take care of the cubs. You must return now, as Megan is still there and will not return until she knows you are safe. Megan and Katrina need you safely at home."

Now she remembered. "Yes, please have Guardian send me back to my house as soon as possible so that you can rescue Megan and Katrina!"

Sara stood up and looked around. She was in a large cavern next to Ituria. "Where should I stand for Guardian to locate me?"

"Go to the middle of the cavern where the light is shining down," Ituria replied. "He will have one of the dragons create the blue light to carry you back to your home."

"Got it!" Sara said as she ran toward the lighted space.

"Sara, if more help is needed, please call to Guardian and ask him to find Knocker," Ituria called to her as she ran.

Nodding to Ituria as she reached the transport point, Sara then shouted out, "Guardian, I am ready. Please send me home!"

A blue light quickly appeared around Sara, and she felt herself being lifted rapidly into the air. The trip back was fast; however, the vortex again caused Sara to lose consciousness.

It was Angela who was able to wake her. "Sara, you must awaken!" Angela called to her in her mind. "We are back, and you must get back inside your house now! The poachers are on their way back!"

Sara heard Angela's voice in her sleep, calling to her. She had to wake up and get back home. The vortex made her so tired, but she knew they were depending on her. She had to get back into the house before anyone noticed she was gone, especially the poachers!

"Yes!" Sara whispered, opening her eyes. "I am awake now." Rubbing her eyes and standing up, she started running to her house. "Please tell Megan and Katrina I'm back and I'm on my way home now!"

Angela responded, "I have done so, they say please hurry and be safe, the poachers are on their way!"

# Chapter Thirteen

# Megan's Promise

Sara could hear someone running in the woods as she slipped in the back door. Quickly locking the door, she went to her room and changed back into her nightgown. Lying down in her bed, she pretended she was sleeping again. Her eyes were closed, but she was listening for any sounds, hoping the poachers would skip her house since they had already been here once tonight.

The familiar pounding on the door returned. "Let me in!" Doug shouted as he banged several times on the door.

Her father woke up and ran first to check to see if Sara was there; she heard his footsteps on the floor outside her room. After confirming she was there, he said with relief, "Thank goodness you're here, Sara! I don't know what's gotten into these men. At least I can say you haven't left since the last time they were here! You stay in your room now, okay?"

"Okay, Father," Sara replied, hoping her father could get rid of Doug once again.

"What do you want this time?" Sara's father yelled through the door, not opening it. "My daughter is still here; my son and I are still here! No one has gone outside tonight!"

"I heard a girl's voice, a young girl, shouting in the woods tonight!" Doug yelled back. "I need to talk to your daughter to see if it was her!"

Sara listened from her bedroom. *They must have heard me call to Guardian!* She was here now, so she could reply that she had not left, her father would back her up. She waited in her room to see which way the conversation went, not wanting to meet Doug again tonight if she didn't have to.

"Let me in now!" Doug screamed. "I need to talk to your daughter! Let me in, or I will break this door down!"

"Okay," Sara's father fearfully said, "just a minute. Let me get the lock." Talking softer so Doug would not hear, he called to his son, Samuel, who was in another room and was standing in the doorway looking at the father. "Samuel, please stay in your room. One less person involved may make this easier, okay?"

"Yes, Father," came the reply as Samuel turned and went back into his room and closed the door. "I will stay in here until you call for me. Please be careful!"

"I will, Son," he replied apprehensively. "I've got to figure out what is going on, and I need to focus on keeping Sara safe now."

"Sara," he called to her as he was unlocking the front door, "please get dressed and come to the front room. The authorities have returned to question you."

"Yes, Father," Sara called from her room.

Letting Doug in the front door, her father said, "I've asked her to change from her night clothes, please wait until she changes and comes out of her room, it will only be a minute."

"Okay," Doug replied angrily, "I'll give her one minute. But no more!"

As she was changing, Angela told her that Megan and Katrina were just outside the house and that they were waiting for Sara to be safe before they would leave.

"Angela," Sara whispered, "tell them they need to escape before the poachers find them! I should be okay, but these men have seen Megan and are looking for her. They need to get away while they can!"

"I have relayed your message to Megan," Angela replied. "Megan said she will not leave until these humans are gone from the area. She promised Knocker that you would be safe, and she keeps her promises."

*I need to get these men to leave now, so Megan can take Katrina home!*

After changing, Sara walked out into the front room. She had two missions at this point—one, to convince Doug that she had not left the house and, two, to get Doug to leave the area so Megan and Katrina could escape. She would do her best to protect her family and Megan from these men, no matter what happened to her!

"Alright, little girl," Doug said as she walked out of her room, "where have you been tonight? Did you leave after I visited earlier?"

"What?" Sara replied, acting surprised. "Why would I do that? You told us not to go out at night. I don't know what is going on out there, but I stayed in my room. What has happened that makes you think we went outside?"

"Well, I heard a young girl yelling a bit ago in the woods, and it sounded like you!" Doug said in a threatening voice. "How do I know you didn't leave after I was here?"

"I have been here the whole night; my father and my brother have been here too. We don't go out at night, you made that clear a few weeks ago when you visited us," Sara replied. Her voice sounded nervous, and she hoped that Doug would think she was scared of him, even though she was more fearful for what he might do to Katrina if he found Katrina and Megan outside.

"I don't believe you!" Doug shouted. "I think you know something, and I'm not going to leave until you tell me!"

"There's nothing to tell!" Sara exclaimed. "You have made it clear we can't go out of our homes at night. We are staying inside like you ordered us to." Not sure where to go with this, she continued, wanting to put Doug on the defensive. "What are you doing outside that you don't want anyone to know about?"

"What I do outside at night is none of your business!" Doug yelled at her. "Now, what were you doing outside tonight? It had to be you; there are no other little girls around here!"

"I don't know what you heard, but it wasn't me!" Sara replied angrily. "You just need to leave and go find what you're looking for somewhere else!"

"Sara," her father said in a frightened voice, "you must not talk to the authorities like that!"

"Why not?" Sara said. "They come here all hours of the night, many nights, just to wake us up and see if we are inside the house. It's time someone asked them why!"

"Listen, little girl…" Doug started in a threatening voice, but then he stopped as they all turned to the door as a female voice started yelling from the other side.

The voice called out, "I hear you in this house. What are you looking for? I'm out here, so leave them alone!"

# Chapter Fourteen

# ANOTHER POTION NEEDED

"Who's that?" Doug shouted as he started out the front door.

Tony was running to the door as Doug stepped outside. "Doug, she's back! She ran up to the door and shouted something and then ran back out to the road! Look!"

Doug and Tony stood together just outside the front door as they located Megan in the moonlight.

Peeking around Doug, Sara could see Megan in her human form standing in the road. Her hands were on her hips, and she was staring at the two men, waiting for them to follow her and get away from Sara's house. She knew that Megan was putting herself in danger to protect Sara, and that she must do something to support Megan, but what? There was one thing she could do, but she needed to be quick!

"Father," Sara whispered, "I am going to hide in my room, I don't want to know what they are doing! You need to lock the door and then go and stay in your room too, okay?"

"Yes, Sara, that is the best thing to do. I'll lock the door, and we'll stay inside our rooms," her father replied.

Sara watched as her father locked and bolted the front door and then whispered to Samuel, who was still in his room, "Samuel, we are locking the front door, do not come out of your room, okay!" After hearing Samuel's response, he went to his room, locking that door also.

Sara ran into her room, but she didn't lock the door. She pulled the vial of invisibility potion out of her pocket and drank the other half. She knew she had to get some help for Megan now!

"Angela, please tell Megan I am going for help!" Sara whispered.

As soon as she was invisible, Sara unlocked the back door and ran into the woods for several hundred yards, and then she shouted into the sky, "Guardian, we need Knocker now!" She hoped that she was far enough away so she wouldn't be heard or that Doug and Tony were too distracted to hear her.

Not waiting for a response, she ran back to the house, circling around outside and went over to Megan.

Sara whispered, "Megan, I am right next to you; I took the rest of the invisibility potion. I've called for Knocker. I am here with Angela, and I will stay with you and Katrina; we are a team and will stand together!"

Megan turned briefly as she smelled Sara nearby, then turned to look back at Doug and Tony. "Sara, I must protect you!" she whispered anxiously. "These humans must be stopped!"

"Hey, little girl, where are my tiger cubs?" Doug yelled angrily from across the front yard as he and Tony walked to her. "What did you do with them?"

"Sara, the translation stone does not work so far away." Megan whispered. "I must wait until they get within ten feet to talk to them."

"I will stand here with you Megan, just let me know what I can do to help!" Sara replied.

"Why aren't you answering me?" Doug demanded.

"Maybe she's scared, Doug," Tony said. "Maybe you could be a little nicer!"

"She don't look scared to me!" Doug replied angrily. "And I'm not going to be any nicer to someone who stole my cubs. They were worth a lot of money to me!"

"You got some explaining to do, little girl!" Doug continued. "You aren't going to be able to run away this time! Tony, why don't you go around and block her so she can't run away, okay?" Doug motioned with his hand for Tony to walk toward the right and get nearer to Megan.

As soon as Megan saw they were within the reach of the translation stone, she called to them. "What are you doing around here? Do you live around here?" She let them know she was not scared in the least nor intimidated by these humans approaching her.

"That's the question I have for you, little girl. What are you doing out here tonight?" Doug asked in a menacing voice. "Shouldn't you be home like all the other good little girls?"

"Why, so you can knock on every door of every house on this road, yelling and scaring the residents?" Megan replied. "I'm the one you are looking for, so why do you do that to the children, scaring them like that?"

"I can do whatever I want, got it! The local authorities give me free rein to do whatever I want, as long as I pay them enough," Doug yelled at her. "And you are just another scared little girl." Doug asked angrily, "But, you know something about my cargo tonight, don't you?"

Doug got closer to her, and Megan put out her arm to make sure Sara, in her invisible form, was staying behind her. "I don't have to tell you anything. However, if you are asking about some baby tigers that were illegally caught and being transported out of the country, I may know something about that." Megan's voice was defiant, she was not going to back down, she was not scared of Doug.

"That's exactly what I'm talking about!" Doug shouted at her. "I knew you were involved. Where are they?"

"I have taken them to a safe place, and you will never find them." Megan said in a pleased voice, smiling at Doug. "So, you may as well just go home. Those cubs are safe from humans like yourself!"

"You are going to tell me where they are, or you aren't going to make it home safely tonight, got it!" Doug threatened angrily.

"You don't scare me, puny human!" Megan retorted. Her temper was showing, she was done dealing with these humans!

A rustling of branches across the road drew attention to a figure emerging from the forest. Appearing from the shadows in his human form, Knocker walked over to stand beside Megan.

Tony moved back over to stand next to Doug, worried about the new visitor. "Hey Doug," he whispered nervously, "this was the same guy from a few weeks ago, remember?"

When Knocker was within a few feet of Doug and Tony, he said, "Good evening, I understand you were looking for me."

# Chapter Fifteen

# CONFRONTATION

"Well, well, well," Doug replied in a nasty tone. "So, you *are* still around, and you finally showed up. I thought you were going to let your little friend take the blame!"

"I would never allow my friends to be harmed, not by the likes of you!" Knocker said, agitated but trying to remain calm.

"Well, I want my cubs back, both the ones you two took tonight, as well as the four you took a few weeks ago, and I want them now!" Doug yelled at him.

"We have had enough of your illegal poaching in this area. These tigers are a protected species, and you are not allowed to touch them, much less kill them and then steal their cubs to sell in foreign countries." Knocker replied confidently, not swayed by Doug's tone. "It will no longer be allowed."

"Well, how are you going to stop it!" Doug asked sarcastically. "Two puny kids aren't going to keep me from making a profit in this area. I've got permission from certain government officials, and that's all I need. I pay them, and they look the other way."

"But *we* will not look the other way, nor will we tolerate your harassment and threatening the local people," Knocker responded sternly. "These people don't know anything; it is only myself and my friend here who know what happened to the tiger cubs."

"Well, I don't have to listen to you and your little friend!" Doug replied. "I can do whatever I want to the locals, and you can't do anything about it!"

"Yes, you do have to listen to us, or we *will* do something about it!" Megan yelled at him. "You will never see those cubs again, only I know where they went!" Megan's anger got the better of her, knowing that Doug was fine with killing the tigers and harassing the humans, as long as he made his money.

"Megan," Knocker spoke softly to her, "you must remain calm, remember. They are not worth your anger."

"Yes, Knocker, you are correct," Megan replied, closing her eyes as she tried to calm herself down.

Angela called to Sara, "Sara, you must lead Megan away from this place before she loses her temper and turns into a dragon! I will tell Knocker what you are doing, so he will know what is happening."

In a few moments, Knocker looked over to where Sara was standing and nodded his head, signaling to her that he agreed with Angela's plan.

Sara gently took hold of Megan's arm and started to pull her back a little. "Angela, tell Megan we are leaving, okay?"

Taking a step forward so he was closer to Doug than Megan was, Knocker continued the conversation. "Doug and Tony, it is time to make some decisions."

Seeing Megan backing away, Doug yelled, "Wait there, little girl, you are not getting away that easy! You're not leaving until I get my cubs back! And why did she call you Knocker? You told me your name was Marcus!"

"Megan, you must leave now. I will continue our discussions with these two humans," Knocker replied, looking at Megan.

Sara kept pulling at Megan's arm, knowing that Knocker needed to get Megan out of the conversation. "Megan, we must go now; let's find Katrina!" Sara whispered softly, so Doug would not hear.

"But I must stay and protect..." Megan started.

"No, Megan, I will protect them." Knocker interrupted her. "You must leave now, please, as this discussion must be between myself and them. You should not be involved." Knocker replied seriously, trying to get Megan to understand she should be leaving.

"Yes, I understand," Megan said, nodding her head. Then she turned to walk away, Sara holding her arm as they went off the road and into the forest.

"We are not going to let her go!" Doug called out angrily. "Tony, go get her back here! I'm not letting her go until I get my cubs back!"

"Tony," Knocker replied calmly, "my advice to you is to let her go, and do not attempt to bring her back. Anything you wanted to discuss with her, you can discuss with me."

Tony looked at Doug and Knocker, not quite sure what was going on. In the second he delayed, Sara wrapped her arms around Megan, holding her close, and she disappeared. Now Sara and Megan were both invisible to the humans.

"Megan, stay with me," Sara whispered. "You are invisible, so they can't see you. We must not move, or they will hear you!"

"Yes, Sara," Megan whispered back. "And I need to share something with you. I have some magic seeds in my satchel. If these humans do not leave, we must put a seed in their mouth so they will become part of the forest. We may need your help to do this since you are invisible."

"Agreed," Sara replied. "Just tell me when!"

"Doug," Tony exclaimed, "she just up and disappeared. I don't see her anymore!"

Doug got closer to Knocker and started screaming at him. "I need her to tell me where the cubs are. Those are my cubs, and I want them back!"

Knocker looked at Doug with an angry stare, his green eyes starting to glow. "They were never your cubs. You stole them and were going to sell them so they could be caged and killed for your profit. We will not let that happen. Your reign of terror must stop!"

"Well, I still have you!" Doug said, glaring back at Knocker. "And they are my cubs, and I will get them back. You are going to tell me where they are now, or you will not make it home tonight!"

Another shadow approached from the forest, and Katrina walked up behind Knocker, then stopped next to him. Doug and Tony stepped back quickly when seeing the large tiger so close; however, Knocker placed his hand on Katrina's back and said, "Greetings, friend. These humans are claiming your cubs as theirs."

Using Knocker's translation stone, she answered Doug's threats with her own. "They were never your cubs, they are mine, and you will never harm them or any tigers here again!"

# Chapter Sixteen

# TIME FOR DECISIONS

"How can you be talking? How can I under-stand you?" Tony stammered, staring at the tiger.

However, Doug started to grab his shotgun, but he wasn't fast enough. Knocker quickly grabbed the gun from Doug's hands, broke it into several pieces, and threw it onto the ground.

"You are in no position to threaten my friends," Knocker said, the anger sneaking into his voice, the green glow coming back to his eyes. "Do not try that again. Do you understand!"

"How did you break my gun?" Doug asked. "Was that a trick?"

"Doug, we need to get out of here!" Tony exclaimed, realizing that things were getting out of their control. "We need to go now!"

"No! No silly trick is going to keep me from get-ting my cubs back! And yes, they are my cubs!" he yelled angrily, looking at Katrina.

Looking at Doug and then at Katrina, Knocker's face relaxed, and he became calm again.

"Katrina, you must leave now," Knocker said without any emotion. "I will deal with these humans as they make their choice."

"What do you mean?" Doug asked. "You will deal with us, what choice?"

"Thank you, I will leave and allow them to make their choice." Katrina turned away, disappearing into the shadows.

Knocker watched attentively as Katrina left, ready to intervene in case Doug decided to follow her. Once she was gone from sight, Knocker replied to Doug's question.

"You have two choices," Knocker said calmly. "You can leave this forest now and never return, or you can stay in this forest forever." He looked at Doug and then Tony. "What is your choice?"

Tony didn't hesitate. "I choose to leave and not come back. Are you with me Doug?"

"No, I am not!" Doug argued. "This kid is not going to tell me what to do!"

"Tony," Knocker asked. "What is your choice? You do not need to be swayed by Doug, as you must make your own decision."

"I will leave and never return to this forest again," Tony said very seriously. "That is my choice."

"Done, I accept your choice and your promise never to return to this forest," Knocker acknowledged. "Please know I take promises very seriously. If you do return, you will have to answer to me. You may leave now, and never return!"

"I'm leaving!" Tony said hastily as he turned toward the truck. "Come on Doug, this is serious, let's go!"

"No, I said I'm not going, and this puny kid can't make me!" Doug replied, glaring at Knocker. "I'm not scared of you!"

"Tony, you have made your choice, and Doug has made his. Please leave now," Knocker said. "You may take the truck with you; Doug will not need it again."

"Doug, come on!" Tony pleaded as he started walking away. "Let's just leave!"

"No, I'm not scared," Doug yelled back. "You go ahead and leave, take the truck if you must. I'm not letting this kid get the better of me!"

"Tony, you must leave, now!" Knocker said calmly, but now it was an order, not a request.

"I'm gone!" Tony said as he ran to the truck. Starting it up, he stepped on the gas and sped down the road to the south. The sound of the truck was soon gone, and the forest was quiet.

"Doug, your decision was to stay here in the forest forever, and I accept that decision," Knocker said solemnly. "You have been watched and judged by the creatures who live in this forest, and they have judged that you are a cruel human, who illegally hunts protected animals. You kill for money and sport, and you

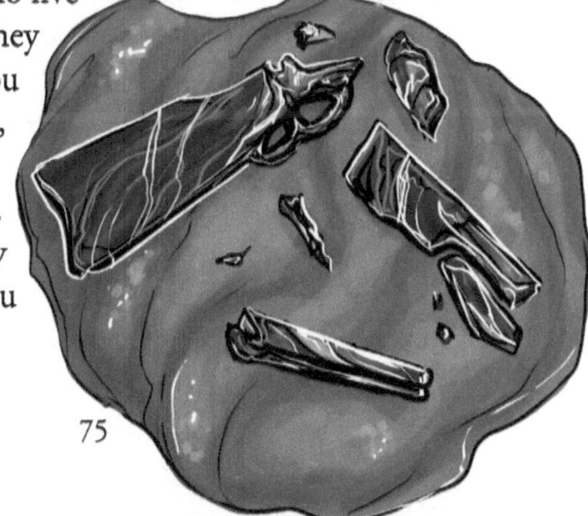

harass and threaten the local humans to further your illegal acts."

"No reason I should stop now! The authorities don't care as long as they get paid," Doug said, still not backing down.

"By your own choosing, you will remain in this forest forever, but you will not be able to harm any of its residents anymore," Knocker continued.

"How are you going to keep me from hunting in the forest? Huh, puny kid?" Doug said sarcastically.

"Well, Doug, that is a very good question," Knocker replied calmly. "But first I must correct your mistaken belief that I am just a puny kid. I'm not sure if a puny kid would have been able to break your gun so easily."

"Yeah, how *did* you do that?" Doug asked, curious now, but still angry. "That was my best gun, killed lots of animals with it. Worked great!"

"And how is killing animals a good thing?" Knocker countered. "You know animals have lives too, right? They have families and homes, children and siblings, just like humans."

"So what!" Doug yelled, "Don't matter to me. I make good money hunting these tigers. Since there are so few in the wild, they bring a good price, especially the live cubs!"

"Yes," Knocker replied then paused, trying to control his anger. "I heard you talking in the market yesterday. You steal and sell the cubs as 'wild tigers' so they can be caged and raised to be slaughtered and their bodies illegally sold as 'wild tiger' parts. You make lots of money that way, you were bragging to others with no thought to how cruel your actions really are. However, you will do this no more; we cannot allow this cruelty to continue!"

Knocker's eyes were glowing bright green now, and his brows were furrowed. Doug looked carefully at Knocker, maybe thinking twice about his decision to stay.

"What's wrong with your eyes, boy?" he asked.

"Megan," Knocker called out. "Are you ready?"

"What do you mean, is she still here?" Doug yelled. "Tony said she disappeared."

Megan stepped away from Sara and became visible again. "Yes, we are ready. We will await your signal."

# Chapter Seventeen

# FINAL RESOLUTION

"**W**hat's going on? Are you ganging up on me?" Doug screamed. "I'm out of here!" Doug took off running into the forest, but he didn't get far.

Megan was watching, and as he started running, she transformed into a dragon and easily caught up with him, blocking him from going further. Megan's teeth were close to Doug's face as she blocked him from escaping; her scales sparkling ruby red in the moonlight.

"You aren't going anywhere!" Megan growled angrily.

"What? What are you? Is this another trick?" Doug stammered. Then he turned around to run the other way and saw Knocker standing right behind him, only a few feet way.

"Do you see this?" Doug exclaimed, not believing he was seeing a dragon. "What is she?"

"That is her true form!" Knocker stated, watching carefully to make sure Doug couldn't slip by him.

"You have chosen to stay in this forest forever, and it is our duty to help you fulfill that promise!"

"No way, I'm leaving now!" Doug said. "And I'll be back with a whole bunch of men to hunt her and you down!"

"No, you will not be leaving!" Knocker said angrily. "You have confirmed your choice. And now, you have just stated that if you are allowed to leave, you plan to come back to harm the creatures of the forest. That was not one of the choices you were given. Therefore, we cannot let you leave!" Taking a few steps back, Knocker instantly turned into a gigantic dragon, even larger than Megan. His blue-green scales shimmered in the moonlight, and he used his large wings to form a wall on both sides of Doug, so he could not run away. Megan did the same; now Doug was trapped!

"You won't get away with this; you won't get away with killing me!" Doug said, trying to argue his way out.

"We don't kill those who need to be punished, that is the human way. We have other ways to deal with cruel humans," Knocker said with authority. "And now we will proceed. Sara, are you ready?"

"Yes, I am." Sara called out.

"So, she was in on this the whole time, I knew it!" Doug yelled. "I'll get you, little girl, you and your whole family! Where are you?"

Sara quietly entered the area where Doug was trapped in the dragon wings. She was still invisible to Doug, who could only hear her voice. His yelling drowned out any soft footsteps she may have made.

Standing silently near him, she waited for the opportunity to place the magic seed in his mouth.

"You know I'm going to get you and your family, right?" Doug yelled, looking around. "But if you help me get away from these monsters now, maybe I'll go easy on you!"

Sara didn't make a sound; she was waiting for the right moment.

"Where did you go!" Doug screamed, starting to panic as all he could see were two angry dragons. "I heard you, little girl, and I will get you. These creatures are too scared to hurt me, so I'll be back!"

Quickly slipping next to Doug as he was yelling, Sara shoved the seed into his mouth. She ran quickly away from him before he realized what was happening, so he could not reach out and grab her.

Walking over to stand by Knocker, Sara responded to his threats.

"Yes, I am protecting the tigers in this area, and you will no longer hurt them or my family!" Sara called out. "You will remain here forever!"

"What is going on… what is…." Doug tried to respond, but the magical seed was transforming him into a part of the forest. His arms stretched out and turned into branches and his feet grew and became roots in the ground. Doug's body stretched and formed a giant tree trunk with many other branches springing out. Within a few minutes, Doug had been totally transformed into a tall tree about forty feet in height. His branches stretched out into the moonlight, full of leaves. He would remain a part of the forest forever!

Megan and Knocker pulled their wings back. The transformation was completed. They had stopped Doug from his illegal hunting!

As Sara looked around, she realized that they were in front of the same den where they had rescued the cubs a few weeks ago, the cubs that had been orphaned by Doug's poaching group who shot and killed the mother tiger. The den had been marked by a lone tall tree left by the loggers. Now there were two tall trees marking the spot in front of the den.

"Doug, do you remember being here a few weeks ago? Here is where you shot a mother tiger who was defending her cubs," Sara called to him. Pointing to the den, she continued, "There is where they were hiding, where they were orphaned by your greed! We were able to rescue them from your illegal and cruel acts!"

Walking closer to the tree, she looked up at the many branches that were now part of Doug. "Doug, you will be here and will see the tigers and other animals in this forest, but they are no longer in danger from your heartless crimes!"

The branches of the tree that was now Doug moved a little, but that was all that Doug was able to do in response to Sara's words.

"One more thing," Sara added. "You need to hope that the illegal loggers don't decide you should be cut down! Now, I must return home!"

# Chapter Eighteen

# HOME AGAIN

"Thank you, Sara, for your assistance in this mission, it is greatly appreciated," Knocker said quietly in Sara's direction. "Please stand back and let me return to my human form, and I will make sure you get home safely."

Sara backed away from Knocker as he crouched on the ground to prepare to turn back into his human form. It took about a minute for Knocker to focus enough to make the transformation from a large dragon back to his small human form.

"Thank you, Knocker, for stopping this poacher from hunting in our forest!" Sara replied once Knocker had change into his human form. "I hope that others like him will stay away so our animals can be safe once again."

"Megan," Knocker called out, "please take Katrina to Ituria's Island. It will be her choice if she and her cubs will return here or stay with Ituria, so please give her the option. I will make sure that Sara gets home safely."

"Yes, Knocker," Megan replied, "I will see you after our mission is completed."

Crouching on the ground, Megan closed her eyes. Knocker and Sara waited quietly as Megan concentrated on transforming. After a few minutes, she was successful in changing back into her human form and ran into the woods looking for Katrina.

"Sara, let's be sure Megan and Katrina make it back," Knocker said softly, listening for sounds in the forest.

"Agreed," Sara replied, "we need to make sure everyone is safe."

Standing in silence, Knocker and Sara waited for the sounds that would confirm their friends were safe. Listening for Megan, they heard a loud roar, and saw a flash of blue light.

Knocker nodded and said, "They are back with Ituria. Now, let's get you home."

"Sara," Knocker commented as he turned in Sara's direction. "I cannot see you, so please follow me closely. I will lead you back to your house."

"Thanks, Knocker," Sara replied. "I left the back door unlocked. I can slip in there and wait in my room until the invisibility potion wears off."

As they got closer to the house, Knocker said, "Sara it was very brave of you to take the invisibility potion to help with our rescue. We have not had someone take it twice in one night, though, so I do not know what the effects may be. You may need to hide in your room for a longer period of time than before."

"That's okay, Knocker," Sara responded. "If I can get into my room, I will just lock it and tell my father I want to keep it locked like I did last time. Hopefully, that will work."

"Okay, that sounds like a good plan," Knocker replied. "We will send Megan back down in a couple of hours to see how things are going. Angela will let you know when Megan has returned."

"Thanks for answering my call for help!" Sara said as she got to the back door of her house. "Knocker, thanks also for helping Megan and Katrina out and for saving our family from the poachers. I am glad that you had a solution to keeping the poachers from hunting in our area, and that they were given a choice. I will let Megan know when all is well. It will be at least few hours before I am visible again."

"Take care, Sara," Knocker said as he got them to her door.

"Take care, Knocker," Sara replied as she opened the back door and slipped inside, locking the bolt from the inside. Quickly stepping into her room, she locked the door and put the chair in front. Hopefully, her father was sleeping by now. She would stay hidden until she was visible again and hoped that it wouldn't take too long.

It was only a few minutes later that she heard a knock at her bedroom door.

"Sara, are you okay?" her father asked. "There was a lot of yelling outside, but it seems to have gone away, and I heard the truck leave a little while ago."

"Yes, Father, I'm fine," Sara responded without opening the door. "Thank you for the information.

I can't hear as much back here as you can from the front of the house. I'm going to keep my door locked just in case they return and break into the house somehow."

"You should be okay, Sara," he replied with concern. "But if that makes you feel better, that's fine. Let's get some sleep, and hopefully, tomorrow will be a better day."

"Yes, Father, I agree," Sara said. "I hope we never see those two around here again!"

"That would be nice, but don't count on it, Sara," her father said. "There is always someone out there willing to hurt others to make money."

"I know, Father, but maybe the animals will win someday!" Sara replied hopefully. "Wouldn't it be nice if people would follow the laws, and the animals had a chance."

"We can always hope, little one, but that isn't the way it normally works," her father said sadly. "Money usually wins."

"Maybe someday it won't!" Sara said positively, reflecting on the events of the night. "Good night, Father! Maybe we won't have to worry about the poachers tonight since you heard them drive away. That will help me sleep better."

"Good night, Sara; sleep well!" her father said, then turned to go back to his room.

Lying on top of her bed waiting to become visible again, she realized how tired she was, and tried to stay awake. However, as time slipped by, and she had not turned visible again, she fell asleep. She was dozing when she heard from Angela.

"Sara, Megan is outside, asking if you are okay," Angela said, waking her from a light sleep. Looking at her hands, Sara was visible again. The mission was complete!

"Thank you, Angela," Sara replied. "Please tell Megan all is well. Please thank her for rescuing the cubs tonight and tell her that I am always available to help!"

"Done," Angela said after a few moments. "Megan thanks you for your valuable help, and she will contact you if another rescue is needed."

Sara held her necklace close. "Thank you too, Angela, you were so helpful tonight, we make a good team!"

"You are welcome, my brave young Sara," Angela replied. "Now, it is time for you to get some rest, you have had a very busy night!"

THE END

*until Sara's next adventure!*

# Note From The Author

Although this is a fantasy adventure, the dangers to tigers are real. The year 2022 was the "Year of the Tiger." In China, the tiger is a highly revered animal for its strength and courage and it is considered to be the king of the jungle. However, there are no more wild tigers in China! They have been systematically killed or poached for the illegal tiger trade. Whenever a tiger does cross the border into China, they are usually poached (illegally hunted and killed).

There are tiger farms where tigers are raised in cages like cattle, and cubs are taken from their mothers almost immediately after birth to promote reproduction of more cubs. Even with this source of tiger parts, the demand for wild tiger parts continues. Over the last 100 years, the number of wild tigers globally has dropped from 100,000 wild tigers to only 4,000 individuals. This great decline is despite tigers being declared an endangered species and laws banning the sale of tiger parts (including, bones, claws, pelts, etc.). These laws are not enforced, and the sale of these products perpetuates.

Loss of habitat, illegal logging, and continual illegal poaching may mean there are no wild tigers left when the next Year of the Tiger gets here in 2034. Will there be any wild tigers left? That depends on how humans act now.

The USA recently passed the Big Cat Public Safety Act that was signed into law on December 20, 2022. This Act severely restricts the possession and exhibition of big cats, including tigers, in the United States. This is a step in the right direction! Please learn about and help protect the few wild tigers that remain, along with the other wild creatures that are struggling just to survive in today's world!

https://leavethemwild.org/will-it-be-the-year-of-the-tiger-its-up-to-you/

https://e360.yale.edu/features/how_tiger_farming_in_china_threatens_worlds_wild_tigers

# BOOK CLUB QUESTIONS

1. How did Sara learn that Megan was waiting for her in the back forest?
2. How were they going to stop the truck that was carrying the tiger cubs?
3. Why did Sara get caught in the cage? How did she keep the poachers from seeing her?
4. Why is the adult tiger following Sara?
5. How does Sara make it home before the poachers get to her house?
6. Why do the poachers come to Sara's house a second time?
7. What happens to Doug after he refuses to leave the forest?
8. What happened to the cubs that were being rescued?
9. What is the current population of wild tigers as compared to 100 years ago? Why is there such a decline?
10. What happens to an ecosystem when you remove the apex (top) predator?
11. Something to think about—If there comes a time when there are no more tigers in the wild, what does that mean for the

ecosystem itself? What can be done now to prevent the extinction of tigers in the wild?

# ABOUT THE AUTHOR

J.B. moved to Florida in her early teens and has lived there ever since, enjoying the mild weather and abundance of wildlife. She even spent several seasons raising orphan squirrels. She graduated from the University of Central Florida and has spent her working career in the legal profession. Her novels are inspired by her family and nature, and she also wants to encourage children to learn and care about the Earth's wild creatures, so they understand that wildlife needs our help to survive in today's world.

www.facebook.com/J.B.Moonstar
Instagram@J.B.Moonstar
Jbmoonstar.author@gmail.com
Website—jbmoonstar.com

# Discover More by JB Moonstar

### Chronicles of Ituria

Russ and The Hidden Voice

Taylor and the Red Wolf Rescue

Jenna and the Legend of the White Wolf

Jenna and the Eyes of Fire

Jan and the Secret Cave

Jan and the Search for Lilya

Taylor and the Final Nine

Michelle and the Missing Manatee

Jenna and the Broken Promise

Sara and the Secret Mission

& More Adventures to Come!

### The Mermaids of Crystal Cay

Kimmi and the Sea Dragon

Roselia and the Ancient Warriors

& More Adventures to Come!

### Coloring Book from

### Artist Jenn Kotick

Mermaids

# Discover more at
# 4HorsemenPublications.com

**10% off using HORSEMEN10**

www.ingramcontent.com/pod-product-compliance
Lightning Source LLC
Chambersburg PA
CBHW031547310726
48971CB00008B/2660